The Berry Bitty
Princess Pageant

GROSSET & DUNLAP
Published by the Penguin Group
Penguin Group (USA) Inc., 375 Hudson Street, New York, New York 10014, USA

USA | Canada | UK | Ireland | Australia | New Zealand | India | South Africa | China
Penguin Books Ltd, Registered Offices: 80 Strand, London WC2R 0RL, England

For more information about the Penguin Group visit penguin.com

ISBN 978-0-448-46691-0   10 9 8 7 6 5 4 3 2 1

The Berry Bitty Princess Pageant

By Mickie Matheis

Illustrated by Laura Thomas

Grosset & Dunlap

An Imprint of Penguin Group (USA) Inc.

It was a busy morning in Berry Bitty City.
Everyone was bustling about doing chores.

Strawberry Shortcake was in the Berry Café baking a batch of scrumptious scones when she heard a commotion in the town square.

She wiped the flour from her hands and walked over to see what the fuss was about.

"What's going on?"
Strawberry asked her friends.
A crowd had gathered to watch
Kadiebug and Sadiebug argue.

"I want to read it!" demanded Sadiebug.

"No, it's my turn!" Kadiebug told her.

"Ladies, it's Bosley's job to read the official decree," said Mr. Longface Caterpillar.

He held in his hands a scroll that unrolled all the way to the ground.

"Humph!" muttered Sadiebug and Kadiebug.

There was a murmur of excitement as Bosley cleared his throat.

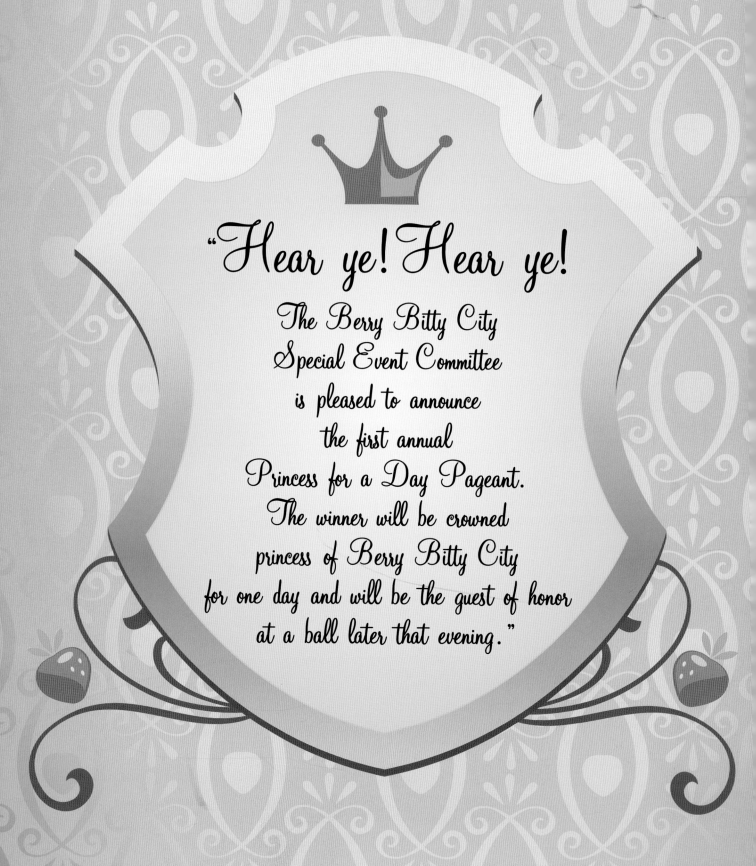

"Hear ye! Hear ye!
The Berry Bitty City
Special Event Committee
is pleased to announce
the first annual
Princess for a Day Pageant.
The winner will be crowned
princess of Berry Bitty City
for one day and will be the guest of honor
at a ball later that evening."

"Princess for a day!

How berry exciting!"

"Princesses wear

beautiful gowns!"

"And sparkly tiaras!"

"What do we have

to do to sign up?"

Mr. Longface explained the rules of the pageant. The girls had to dress up in a costume, give a short speech, and perform a special talent.

The winner would be chosen by a panel of judges—Jadeybug, Berrykin Bloom, and Mr. Longface.

"That sounds like fun," said Cherry Jam.

"And a lot of work," Plum Pudding pointed out.

"Then we'd better start getting ready," Strawberry said. "Let's go!"

The girls spent the next few days preparing for the pageant. Raspberry Torte quickly finished designing and sewing her costume.

It was beautiful!

"But what will I do for my talent?" she wondered aloud. "I don't have any ideas."

Meanwhile, Lemon Meringue had decided on the perfect hairstyle for the pageant. "Of course, it doesn't matter how nice my hair looks if I don't have a costume to go with it," she thought.

"Your dance routine looks great, Plum," said Cherry. The two girls were at the Sweet Beats Studio, working on their talent performances.

"And that new song you wrote is my favorite one yet!" Plum complimented her friend. "It really got my toes tapping."

"I wish I could write a speech as easily as I can write a song," Cherry said.

Plum nodded. "I know. I haven't even started mine."

A few days before the pageant, the girls gathered at the Berry Café for a smoothie break. They talked about their pageant preparations.

"I have my speech written. That's all I've done," Blueberry Muffin shared.

"You're further along than I am," Orange Blossom admitted. "I'm worried that I won't be ready for the pageant."

"I think we're all behind," Lemon said, to cheer her up.

Strawberry thoughtfully sipped her smoothie. "You know, getting ready for the princess pageant should be fun," she said. "Maybe it would be better if we stopped working separately and worked together instead."

"That's a fruitastic idea!" exclaimed Lemon.

"Yes!" agreed Raspberry. "I can design the costumes."

"And we can help everyone with their talent performances," said Plum and Cherry.

"Exactly," Strawberry agreed. "We're all good at different things. So let's pitch in to help each other become the best princesses possible!"

The next day, all the girls
gathered at Raspberry's boutique
to work on their costumes.

Raspberry gave Orange a list of things she needed,
and Orange ran to her store to fill a box with fabric and
feathers, buttons and bows, and sequins and ribbons.

As Raspberry and Orange worked on the costumes, Lemon styled the girls' hair. In no time at all, the costumes and hairstyles were complete.

"We look great!" the girls chorused as they admired themselves in the mirror.

Next, the girls sat in a circle around Blueberry. Strawberry read a silly speech about her pets, Pupcake and Custard, and everyone laughed. Blueberry suggested a few ways to make the speech even funnier. Soon all the speeches were prepared.

After that, Plum and Cherry helped their friends perfect their talent performances.

"Nice job, girls!" Cherry said, clapping enthusiastically.

"I think we're ready!" Strawberry said. "Princess pageant—here we come!"

On the day of the pageant, the townspeople filled the square.
They enjoyed the glamorous costumes and heartfelt speeches, but they
were really captivated by the talent performances.

Plum's dancing and Cherry's singing had the crowd swaying and
humming along. Blueberry shared a story she had written. Orange
built an amazing miniature Berry Bitty City out of blocks.

Raspberry created a beautiful arrangement of fruits and flowers.
Lemon styled the fur of Pupcake and Custard, and paraded them
around the stage. Last but not least, Strawberry baked a huge layer
cake in the shape of a princess crown, using the biggest, juiciest
berries as jewels.

When it came time to announce the winner, Postmaster Bumblebee said, "All the ladies were lovely and elegant. But we can only have one Princess for a Day—so please join me in congratulating Miss Strawberry Shortcake!"

The townspeople cheered loudly—but none louder than Strawberry's berry own best friends!

Strawberry stepped to the front of the stage. Mr. Longface put a tiara on her head, and Jadeybug tied a bright pink sash around her. Although she smiled at the crowd, Strawberry felt a little worried inside. What if her friends were upset because they hadn't been chosen? After all, each girl had worked very hard and had done her berry best.

Suddenly, she had a great idea. "Thank you!" Strawberry said to the crowd. "I'm so honored to be your Princess for a Day. Please join me at the ball tonight."

That night at the ball, Princess Strawberry made an announcement. "As Princess for a Day, I would like to ask Kadiebug and Sadiebug to read my first official decree."

"In honor of all the work that everyone put into making the pageant so much fun, Princess Strawberry proclaims that all of her friends get to be princesses, too!"

Strawberry's friends gasped and looked at each other in delight. Berrykins, carrying pretty tiaras on pillows, marched into the ballroom and stood next to Strawberry. One by one, Strawberry placed a tiara on the head of each of her friends.

"My second order of business is to declare the first annual Princess for a Day Pageant a berry sweet success!" declared Strawberry. "Now let's have a royal good time."

And with that, Strawberry and her fellow
princesses happily danced the night away—
princesses for a day, berry best friends forever!